A Tale of Forgiveness and Love

by

Daisy M. Bratcher

DORRANCE PUBLISHING CO
EST. 1920
PITTSBURGH, PENNSYLVANIA 15238

Dorrance Publishing Co
585 Alpha Drive
Pittsburgh, PA 15238
Visit our website at *www.dorrancebookstore.com*

ISBN: 979-8-8852-7106-6
eISBN: 979-8-8852-7833-1

Chapter 1

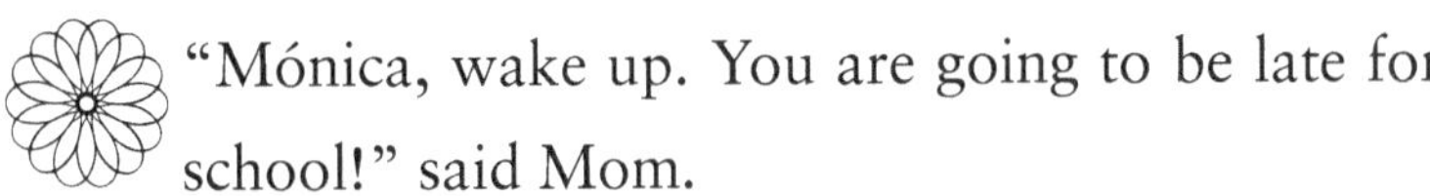"Mónica, wake up. You are going to be late for school!" said Mom.

"Mom, do I have to go? Can't I stay here with you and help you do chores? My stomach hurts just to think that I must face Sandra. You know how mean she has been to me all year. Can't I just stay home?"

Her mother just looked at her with a sad face. She knew the whole year had been a struggle for Mónica. However, school was important, and she couldn't risk having Mónica flunk.

Mónica was such a sweet and loving child, and it was so unfair that she was treated so badly at school. Mónica had a beautiful voice and she loved to sing, however, the only one that was privileged enough to hear her sing was her mom. She was far too shy to share her gift with anyone else. Mónica would sing especially when she was sad, which unfortunately was almost every day when she came home from school. Her mom was very concerned. She wanted Mónica to excel in school and have many friends, but it didn't look like this would be happening any time soon. What could she possibly do to help her?

While Mom was busy preparing breakfast for her family, Mónica very reluctantly got up and took a shower to change her mood. It was funny how something so simple could change her mood and make her feel like a spring morning all fresh and sweet. She got out of the shower and put on her school uniform and carefully brushed her long silky black hair. She looked at herself in the mirror; she couldn't understand why the kids picked on her. She didn't bother anyone, she didn't speak out of turn, and she certainly tried not to draw attention to herself, yet the kids still found a way to make her life miserable. They called her "pocha" and "gringa" and other hurtful names because she was born in the US and teased her because she spoke Spanish with an accent and mainly spoke English, as if speaking another language made her come from outer space.

She looked closely at herself. She looked as normal as any other kid. Her eyes were even, she had a small dainty little nose, her mouth was always curved into a smile, especially when she was around her family. Her head didn't look bigger than the rest of the kids. What was it that made them hurt her so much?

She was deep in thought when her mother called out her name again from the kitchen.

"Mónica, hurry up! It is almost time for school, and you haven't had your breakfast!"

"I am almost done, Mom; I am just braiding my hair. I will be right down.

Mónica finished brushing her hair and picked up her backpack with her school things. How she dreaded to face Sandra. Sandra had been a bully since first grade, and she was relentless. She always picked on Mónica and Rosario, her best friend, because they were both quiet and shy and would stay away from the other children who sided with Sandra at recess.

Fourth grade was difficult. The only thing that Mónica liked about fourth grade was her teacher, Miss Sánchez. Miss Sánchez was a wonderful teacher! She was very caring and nice, and she always stood up for Mónica. Maybe that is why Sandra was so mad at her. Miss Sánchez always told Mónica that maybe Sandra was so mean because she had problems at home. Yet, it wasn't Mónica's fault, so why did she take it out on Mónica? Miss Sánchez told Mónica to try to be nice to Sandra and that maybe she would change her attitude towards her. But how could she do it? Sandra didn't give her a chance to make friends with her, and to be honest, even if she did, Mónica wasn't so keen on being the friend of a bully anyway.

Mónica went into the kitchen where she found the rest of her family. She was the eldest of five children. Her siblings were two girls Elena and Sara and two boys Efren and Carlos. Her mom was Sofía, and her dad had recently passed away in a car accident coming home from work when they lived in Houston. Her mom had been left with five young children to raise by herself, so she decided to move to Puerto Vallarta, Mexico for work. Fortunately, her mom had studied to be an architect and worked at a prestigious firm, where she had friends she had made at the university. But that didn't make it any easier for her. Her parents had passed away long ago, and she didn't have any siblings or other relatives she could reach out to, to help her. The children had to go to day care after school so that she could work for long hours at the firm.

Mónica was only ten and her siblings were nine, seven, five and one. Her poor mom had more than she could handle. Elena was the opposite of Mónica; she was always in some kind of mischief. Efren, the oldest of the two boys, loved to dismantle things and then put them back together. Once he had tried to fix Mom's watch and had several pieces left over when he finished. He was always very interested to know how things worked. Mónica smiled as she thought of her brother; he was the one that was more like their dad. Then there was Carlitos, the baby. He was such a cute and loving little guy. He had just turned one and was walking, or should she say running? That little guy ran very fast, especially if he had been caught trying to get into the dishwasher! Yes, Mom had her hand's full, and she was very determined to raise her children properly and help them become the people they were supposed to be, with or without a father.

Her dad had passed away without leaving them any kind of protection and life was hard. His untimely death had depleted their savings and now they were behind in paying for everything. Fortunately, the house they lived in was theirs and it was paid for, so they didn't have to worry about that. But there were bills to pay and hardly any money to pay them with. Mom had to work very hard to make ends meet.

The firm where her mother worked was very good to her and made special concessions for her at times, especially when the younger kids were ill. The day care they attended was also government subsidized so she didn't have to pay for that either. However, having five young children to feed and clothe was still a challenge and the death of her husband had only been six months ago.

Mónica worried about her mom and about how hard she worked and how tired she always was. She tried to help her as much as she could, but at her young age there wasn't much she could do to help. So, she really tried to be good at school to not cause any more grief for her mom, but Sandra didn't make it easy for her.

Mónica sat down at the table where her mother had placed a plate of chilaquiles made with a green hot sauce which was her favorite. Next to the chilaquiles were a couple of over easy eggs and a glass of fresh orange juice. Her mom was a great cook and in Mónica's opinion, the best cook in the whole wide world.

"Mónica," her mom said bringing her out of her thoughts. "When you come home from school today, I want you to pick up Carlitos from the neighbor's and take care of him until I get home from work. Can you do that please?"

"Yes, Mom."

Mónica ate her breakfast as quickly as she could and left for school. She had to walk quite a ways, so she hurried.

Chapter 2

As Mónica walked to school, she thought about her surroundings. She and her family lived in Puerto Vallarta, Mexico which is in the state of Jalisco. Jalisco is known for its delicious food, people with beautiful eyes and colorful songs performed by Mariachis. As in all Mexico, the people were usually very happy despite their needs. People had to work hard to make a good living and things were expensive, but they managed to have time to spend with family and friends and have a good time.

Puerto Vallarta was a magical place. The people were very warm and friendly and in the most part very accepting of others and their differences. Here people could feel right at home even if they were only staying for a few days. The city was modern yet there was still a warm and cozy small town feeling where people still cared for each other. The city was growing a lot and many people came to vacation here. There were always a lot of tourists and many of them (Canadians and Americans) came back to live once they experienced the warmth of the people and the beautiful beach. The boardwalk was very nice with shops all along its way. There were also many restaurants that enticed people to come in and eat. The food prepared in these restaurants was to die for. They had, of course, a great variety of Mexican dishes but they also catered to those that were unfamiliar with Mexican cuisine. The servers were very gracious and kind and very interested in providing their customers with excellent service and a fun atmosphere. When the sun set, people would come out after work to hear the Mariachis play and would sing along with their songs. Yes, Puerto Vallarta was a great place to live.

Mónica was happy she lived in Puerto Vallarta because she was close to the beach and on the weekends if Mom didn't have to work, they would go to the beach and swim in the ocean. That was so much fun! She really liked spending time with her mom.

Her mom would tell her stories about far off places, where people were sweet and kind to each other. She would have liked to live in such a place where there were no bullies and mean people. But as Mom always said, "You can't live in a fairy tale."

She was deep in thought when she got to school. She didn't see Sandra coming towards her. Sandra was a little older than Mónica. It was said that her parents were divorced and that she and her siblings didn't spend much time with their father. That was sad; Mónica felt sorry for her. The funny thing was that Sandra made fun of Mónica because she didn't have a father and yet she had a father that wasn't there for her even if he was alive. There was such bitterness in Sandra.

Mónica wished she could do something for her, but how could she approach Sandra? How does one befriend a bully?

Sandra was a tall, chubby girl with short, dark brown hair. She was smart, and she was not bad looking. She had been put back a year after her parents divorced because of all the chaos that was going on in her life. That's why she was in Mónica's class.

"Hey! Watch where you're going!" said Sandra.

"I'm sorry, Sandra. I didn't see you coming," said Mónica.

"Well, you better get some glasses. You'll look even dumber—ha-ha!" Sandra laughed.

Sandra walked away leaving Mónica upset and wishing she didn't have to be in the same classroom with her. Why? Why was she so mean to her?

Mónica walked in her classroom as the bell rang. Her teacher was writing something on the board.

"Oh, hi, Mónica! I didn't hear you walk in," said Miss Sánchez. "Did you have a nice weekend? I bet you went to your favorite place in the world, right?"

"Yes, I did, Miss Sánchez. Mom took us to the beach, and we spent most part of the day swimming. Later we went to Don Pedro's for lunch and later she took us to the movies. We saw a wonderful movie about a dog who was lost and found its way home! It was great! How was yours?"

"Mine was good, although I didn't have as much fun as you did. I spent almost all weekend grading papers."

As Miss Sánchez finished saying that, the children began to pour in. Mónica's heart sank as she saw Sandra take her seat behind her. She had that smirk on her face that told Mónica that she was about to do something to her.

Miss Sánchez greeted the class and asked them to turn to page five of their math books. They would be studying math problems and how math was used in everyday life and in everything we did without us even noticing it.

Miss Sánchez put a simple story problem on the board and asked Mónica to come up front to solve it. As Mónica got up, she fell back onto her chair. Sandra had tied her braids to the back of her chair. When Mónica fell back, everyone in the classroom was laughing at her, with the exception of course of Miss Sánchez. When Mónica tried to get up she fell again, this time she fell flat on her face. The children roared with laughter. Miss Sánchez hurried to help untie her braids and help Mónica up.

"Ok, who did this?" asked Miss Sánchez.

Sandra looked innocently at Miss Sánchez and said, "Her braids are so long that they probably got stuck and she fell." No one said anything in fear that Sandra would retaliate.

"Sandra, come into the hall with me for a second."

Sandra got up and as she passed Mónica's desk she kicked her causing Mónica to burst into tears. Miss Sánchez saw that fortunately and grabbed Sandra by the arm and took her out of the classroom and straight to the principal's office.

"Mr. Pérez, I caught Sandra kicking Mónica again. She is constantly picking on her and causing her to miss school. Would you please call her parents and have them talk with their daughter? This can't continue to happen."

Mr. Pérez looked at Sandra thoughtfully. "What do you have to say for yourself, Sandra? Is this true?"

Sandra looked first at Miss Sánchez with disgust and then looked at Mr. Pérez who was waiting for her response. "Mónica had her foot out and I tripped over it. She should be the one here not me!"

"Miss Sánchez, go back to your classroom. I will handle this."

Miss Sánchez returned to the classroom and found the children still laughing and making fun of Mónica.

"Ok, children settle down. I will not tolerate any more bad behavior in my classroom. If you have anything against Mónica you can talk it out with her in a respectful manner. From now on anyone who disrupts our class again will be sent to the principal's office without question. Do you understand?"

"Yes, Miss Sánchez," they said in unison.

Miss Sánchez went over to Mónica's desk and gave her a big hug saying, "Mónica, if you are ok now, will you please come up front to solve the problem?"

"Yes, Miss Sánchez," said Mónica, wiping away her tears.

In the meantime, Mr. Pérez was talking with Sandra's mother who had had to leave work to come to the principal's office.

"Mrs. Saldivar, your daughter is causing a lot of problems and is picking on helpless, shy children who are afraid to get hurt by your daughter. Before I expel her, I want to understand the situation at home and find the cause for such behavior."

Mrs. Saldivar bowed her head in shame. She was aware that Sandra had changed since she and her father had divorced. Sandra spent a lot of time by herself because she had to work late hours to make ends meet. It had been difficult, and her ex-husband was not helping as he should.

"Mr. Pérez. I am so sorry about this. Sandra is lashing out and acting like this since my husband and I got divorced. It has affected her more than we had ever thought. Please don't expel her, I will find the means to have her see a therapist."

"Mrs. Saldivar," said Mr. Pérez, "I expect you to take care of this immediately or else I will have to expel Sandra. Good day."

Mrs. Saldivar walked out with Sandra. Sandra looked quite satisfied with the outcome. She didn't want to stay at school anyway. Miss Sánchez was boring, and she cared for no one except for Mónica. She was glad that she had tripped Mónica, and she would not apologize no matter what.

Mrs. Saldivar was quiet all the way home. She didn't know what to say to Sandra that would help her change her attitude and behavior at school.

That day, as Mónica walked home from school, she sang a sad song. She always did this when she was sad and didn't know what to do. She had a very sweet voice and was able to sing high notes. She didn't realize that Miss Sánchez was behind her and had heard her sweet song. Miss Sánchez promised herself that she would ask Mónica to sing at the school's anniversary celebration the following week. It was going to be hard because she was so shy, but she would give it a try.

When Mónica's mom got home from work that night and was tucking Mónica in, she asked Mónica how her day had been. Mónica burst into tears and said she was never, ever going back to school, that Sandra was picking on her constantly and she was sick of it.

"I hate school, Mom! Why can't I stay here and be home schooled?"

"You know why, Mónica. I don't have the time. I must work long hours to put food on our table and pay for other things. I can't afford to lose my job."

Mónica covered her face with her blanket. She knew how much her mom had to work and all the sacrifices she made to raise her and her siblings. She would just have to try her best to manage.

"I know, Mom. I will keep trying to make friends with Sandra and maybe that way she will stop being such a bully."

"That's right, Mónica. You always have a choice. You can be resentful and mean or you can choose to be kind and forgiving and try to understand why she is the way she is. You need to speak up. You need to find common ground with her and try to reason with her. People are not always what they seem to be."

Mónica thought a minute about what her mom said and started thinking of ways to confront Sandra without making it worse.

That night a lot of thoughts went through her mind. Sandra couldn't be so mean. Why was she acting that way? How could she help her be different? She would talk to Miss Sánchez; maybe between the two of them they could come up with a plan to help Sandra.

Mónica closed her eyes and went fast to sleep. Tomorrow would be a better day; she was sure of it.

Chapter 3

When Mónica arrived at school that day, she didn't see Sandra and wondered where she was. She approached Miss Sánchez to ask her about Sandra. Miss Sánchez said that she had been suspended for a few days so she could think about her behavior. Mónica remembered that she needed Miss Sánchez to give her ideas as to what they could do to make things better.

"Miss Sánchez, what can we do to help Sandra change?" said Mónica.

"What do you mean, Mónica?"

"Well, my mom says that maybe Sandra is such a bully because she has problems at home that she doesn't know how to solve. She says that I need to find something good in her and build a relationship around that that could help her be different."

"Mónica, this girl has been mean to you for over a year. Are you sure you want to help her? Why?"

"I guess I feel sorry for her. Mom says that she heard from Sandra's mother that she really misses her dad and that he is not there for her. I just don't want her to be sad or angry anymore. Can you help me come up with a plan to help her?"

"Yes, of course if that is what you really want."

"Yes, it is," said Mónica.

"Okay then, let's see. I heard that she likes to play the violin and that she is quite good at it. Maybe you two could do something together at next week's celebration. Why don't you go with me to her house and talk with her? Maybe this just might do the trick!"

That afternoon when school was over, Mónica and Miss Sánchez walked over to Sandra's home. Miss Sánchez knocked at the door and Sandra answered it. She was stunned to see not only Miss Sánchez but Mónica as well.

"What do you want? If you have come to lecture me or make me apologize to Mónica, forget it. I won't," said Sandra.

Miss Sánchez smiled and said, "No, Sandra. This is not why we are here. May we come in?"

Sandra opened the door wide enough for them to enter. It was a nice house. It was made of red brick, and it had a jacaranda tree in the front patio that was in full bloom. The home was furnished in colonial style and had rustic furniture. Sandra showed them into the living room and the maid offered them something cold to drink since it was so hot outside.

Sandra asked them to sit and waited for Miss Sánchez to tell her why they were there.

"As you know, next week we are celebrating the school's 50th anniversary and every class has to perform. It can be a solo, duet or the participation of the whole class. I have a confession to make before I say anything else.

"The other day, when the incident happened between you and Mónica, I overheard her singing on the way home. I was trying to catch up with her to give her her homework she had left in the classroom, but instead I was so caught up in her song that I forgot and just followed her without her noticing."

Mónica blushed. She had not seen or heard Miss Sánchez behind her otherwise she wouldn't have sung.

Miss Sánchez continued. "Mónica has a beautiful voice and I know that you play the violin very well and thought that perhaps you two could do something together for that occasion. What do you think?"

Sandra was surprised. Why in the world would she ever want to do something with Mónica?

Mónica spoke up before Sandra had a chance to respond. "Sandra, I know that you don't like me, and I don't know why. I have never done anything to hurt you or cause you grief. Can we put all this aside and if not be friends, at least get along and do this? I know that I couldn't do it by myself because I am too shy, but if you help me, I know I can do it."

"You are asking for my help?" asked Sandra not believing her ears.

"Yes, please do this with me. We could practice after school in our classroom with Miss Sánchez and we could be ready for the celebration next week!" said Mónica.

"What do I get out of this?" asked Sandra.

"For starters you won't get expelled and I am sure that you two will have lots of fun performing together," said Miss Sánchez.

I'll think about it and let you know.

Miss Sánchez and Mónica stood up, thanked Sandra for her time and left.

During the walk back, Mónica asked Miss Sánchez, "Do you think she will do it?"

"I don't know, Mónica. She is a tough one."

Mónica also felt insecure; she wasn't sure she could face a whole assembly. What if the students laughed at her? If that happened, she would never go to school in her life!

Miss Sánchez felt the uneasiness in Mónica and asked, "Are you nervous about performing? You shouldn't be, you have a beautiful voice, and it is about time you showed it off."

Mónica wasn't so sure or as confident as Miss Sánchez appeared to be. But as someone said in a movie, "Courage is not the absence of fear." So, she guessed it was okay to feel fear. She would practice and practice for the big day.

In the meantime, Sandra was battling with her own thoughts and fears; deep down she was just as insecure as Mónica and being a bully was just a front she put up so she would never be hurt again, by anyone. She would never trust anyone again and would not let anyone in her life.

She had to admit that it took a lot of guts for Mónica to show up at her home and even talk to her. Deep down she wished she could be more like Mónica, but she was so hurt she didn't know if she could ever be like that again.

She would really have to think long and hard about the invitation to participate at the assembly.

Chapter 4

Two days went by and Mónica had not heard from Sandra. Time was closing in real fast, and they had not practiced. Mónica and Miss Sánchez were in the classroom practicing Mónica's song when lo and behold, they saw Sandra come in. They couldn't believe their eyes!

"You're here, Sandra! Thank you so much for coming," said Mónica.

"Don't make it more than it is," responded Sandra. "I'm here because I can't be expelled."

Miss Sánchez looked at both girls. She felt that music was their common ground and that this would be beneficial to them. She smiled and said, "Ok then, let's start practicing. Sandra, I see that you brought your violin. Good thinking."

"The song you will be performing is a lullaby about friendship and love," said Miss Sánchez. "Here is the music sheet. As you can see there is a short intro with the violin and then Mónica starts to sing. Any questions?"

"No," said Sandra. "Let me get my violin out and try the intro."

Sandra took out her violin and played the intro. It was the sweetest sound Mónica and Miss Sánchez had ever heard. Sandra played the violin with such feeling that she almost made them cry. Mónica couldn't believe this was the same girl that caused her so much grief. As Mónica started to sing to the melody, it was Sandra's turn to be impressed. Mónica had a very sweet voice and touched Sandra's heart to the core.

They both stopped and looked at each other not knowing what to do next. Miss Sánchez stood up and went to them and hugged them both saying, "Girls, that was beautiful. You will be a hit and our class will be so proud. Too bad this is not a competition because if it were you two would win!"

Neither girl said anything; they were both shocked and too bewildered to say or do anything. Practice time was over, and it was time to go home and continue practicing there. On the way home, both girls kept thinking about each other and the fact that they had music in common and maybe, with time, they could even become friends. Both shook their head in disbelief.

Miss Sánchez was also thinking of them and the miracle that had just happened. Music was melting Sandra's heart and making Mónica more secure as she heard Sandra play with such mastery. Maybe Sandra wasn't so tough after all and maybe, just maybe, she could help Sandra with whatever it was that was bothering her. What Sandra needed was a mentor and a friend and she would see to it that she became just that for her, no matter what it took. If she could make a positive and lasting impact on one child's life, it would later be passed down in kind.

That night Miss Sánchez went to bed feeling grateful and happy for what had transpired. There was no better feeling than rescuing the shy and also the troubled so they could finally be happy and fulfilled. Wasn't that what teachers were meant to do?

The following afternoon as Mónica and Sandra practiced, she felt them getting closer. There was even a shared moment of laughter between them. Miss Sánchez had taken them treats to eat after practice and even walked them home. The song was coming out wonderful; you could feel the beautiful spirits of these wonderful girls who had so much in common and yet they were so different.

The days went by quickly, as they tend to do, and before they knew it, it was the day of the assembly where the celebration would take place. Since it was a big occasion, parents and families were all invited to attend, and they were to wear their Sunday best to the event. The girls performing were to dress one in blue and the other in pink with their hair styled with curls flowing to their shoulders. That would be a little tricky since Sandra had shorter hair, but her mom managed to style it very nicely.

The event was to be held at 6:00 p.m. at the great hall. The people were starting to arrive and so did the girls. They looked beautiful, you guessed it! Mónica wore the pink dress and Sandra the blue. They arrived almost at the same time and so did Miss Sánchez who lingered back to say hello to the parents of some of her students. She saw how Mónica and Sandra threw themselves into each other's arms laughing and wishing the other good luck in the performance. Miss Sánchez had to refrain from bursting into tears. They had made it! There had been no apologies offered, however, music had softened Sandra's heart and Mónica's sweet spirit had helped Sandra change. There was hope for Sandra!

When she was able to slip away, she approached the girls who were deep into practice and had not noticed her walk in. "Girls, you are next after fifth grade. Mónica, don't look at anyone, pretend that you are walking home and singing this beautiful song and that there is no one there to hear you. Look up and out and everything will be just fine. Sandra, you too. Pretend you are home playing for your mom, and you will do just great. I know you can do it, and girls, let me tell you how proud I am of you! Now go and impress these people!"

Mónica heard the principal announce their song and she and Sandra walked out to the stage, hand in hand. That night they sang and played as if they were angels, and the people could feel something special happening. Love and friendship were blossoming just as the song they performed talked about. When their performance had ended, there was not a sound heard in the hall; their audience was overtaken with amazement. Suddenly they all stood up and burst into applause. They had done it!

As the days went by, nothing was said between them. There was no need; each had communicated through their spirits. There were no apologies, no resentments, no judgements, just two little girls who had gone through many struggles and had found friendship, love, and forgiveness along the way, not just with each other but with a wise teacher who cared enough about her students to make the difference.

Chapter 5

Miss Sánchez sat at her desk thinking back on the school's celebration and how beautifully Mónica and Sandra had performed. They had come a long way during the past few weeks as they came closer to fulfill an assignment. She wondered how she could use this experience to help other kids who were struggling from being bullied. If children only knew how deeply the children they bullied were hurt. How could she help her class, at least, understand the harm and sorrow they were inflicting?

As she sat in front of her computer, she started to browse the internet; perhaps there was something out there she could use to help her class understand the importance of being kind and understanding, of having compassion and empathy for those who are different from themselves. There are many reasons why children can be different; maybe they are from other countries and don't speak the language, maybe they come from low-income families or are quiet because they come from broken homes, or they have mothers who are single parents. Maybe they have recently had someone very near and dear to them die. There are many situations we don't know about that they may be facing.

Some children are abused and neglected at home; they are misunderstood and are not loved or wanted. They are sent to school unkempt, dirty and/or with wrinkled and torn clothes. It is certainly not their fault, yet they are judged and mistreated for their appearance and made fun of by other children. How could she possibly address this issue in a kind and loving way, yet in a firm manner to not allow, ever again, for children to be bullied, at least not in her classroom.

She looked and looked for articles she could share as part of a project she would have her students do to help them understand and prevent bullying. After much reading, she found an article that touched the subject in a very clear and straight forward way.

Yes, she thought. *This will be perfect and since Món-ica and Sandra are getting along so nicely now, I will ask them to lead this project talking about how each of them suffered during the time they had been in the situation of being a bully and the bully's victim.* It would be hard to do because she knew that Mónica didn't like to speak in class and Sandra would be embarrassed to admit before the whole class that she had been a bully. But now she had changed and was very remorseful for what had happened, and Miss Sánchez was sure she would be willing to make amends.

She would make copies of the article for each of her students and after they read it as a class, she would then ask the girls to come to the front of the classroom and talk about their experiences, feelings, and ideas to deal with bullying.

She loved each and every one of her students and would not continue to allow anyone to be hurt again in her classroom. She knew that she had to stop this kind of behavior before it got out of hand and her students became hardened and cruel.

She went to bed that night satisfied with her idea. She only hoped that the message would be well received and followed. She felt peace in her heart knowing that this subject was even more important to teach than any of the other subjects taught. This is something that needed to be taught in the home also, but unfortunately there were many adult bullies out there who had never been taught otherwise and that is what they taught their children from one generation to the next. What a tragedy!

Her eyes were tired from all that reading but she was grateful she had found something that would benefit her students.

The next day, Miss Sánchez woke up early. She needed to get to school to make enough copies of the article she had found the night before. It was a beautiful day; the sun was out, and it felt good to walk in the warmth of the sun. It was late spring, and the flowers were in full bloom and there were birds chirping in the trees and all the sleepy creatures were starting to come out of their winter habitats. This was her favorite time of the year; everything was so colorful and made her feel happy.

She arrived at school, left her things in her classroom, and went directly to the office where she would make copies of the article. On her way to the office, she met the principal in the hallway.

"Good morning, Mr. Pérez. Isn't this the most beautiful day you have ever seen?" greeted Miss Sánchez.

"Ah, Miss Sánchez, you are always so cheerful. Yes, the day is beautiful indeed. Why are you so happy this morning if I may ask?" said Mr. Pérez.

"Well, it turns out that I think I have found a way to keep bullying down to a minimum if not do away with it all together," said Miss Sánchez with a twinkle in her eyes.

"Really, how's that?" asked Mr. Pérez.

"I was thinking very hard last night on how I could help children understand bullying a little better and I found this article that really resonated with what I want to do," said Miss Sánchez handling Mr. Pérez the article she had printed.

"I was just going to the office to make copies for my students to read as a class during our first period and then I was thinking of having them do some more research on the subject at home and then I would have Sandra and Mónica talk about how it has affected them. What do you think?"

"I think that is an amazing idea. Please let me know how it all turns out and if I can be of any help at all. If you have a good experience, maybe we could use this as a project the whole school could do. Nice work, Miss Sánchez!" said Mr. Pérez patting Miss Sánchez on the back.

Miss Sánchez made her copies and headed back to her classroom. She had made a draft of her thoughts for the project and couldn't wait to share it with her class.

The bell rang and her students came trickling in. The last to come in were Mónica and Sandra who were still talking and laughing as they walked in. They both walked to their seats and Miss Sánchez began her class.

"Boys and girls. Today instead of science for our first period, we are going to talk about a subject that is very important for you to learn and apply. As you all have been aware, there had been a lot of conflict between two students in our classroom and now that the conflict has been resolved. I would like to take this experience for us to learn from. Before I continue, I would like to ask their permission to continue as it affects them both." She looked over to where Sandra and Mónica were sitting and they both nodded.

"Ok then. Last night as I was grading some papers, I felt very concerned about the situation and although this one has had a happy ending, not all these situations do, and I would like for us to read this article as a class and come up with some ideas as to how to prevent it and have more love and empathy toward those who are different from us for whatever reason.

Mónica and Sandra, would you please help me pass out these copies? Thank you."

Mónica and Sandra got up from their desks and took the papers from Miss Sánchez. Once all the students had their copy, Miss Sánchez continued.

"We will start reading first with David and then continue to the last row ending with Alma," said Miss Sánchez. The children started to read and pretty soon they were all engrossed in their reading. Miss Sánchez followed along and made corrections as needed explaining the words they didn't understand.

Once the reading was done, first she asked if they had any questions and then she continued. "I would first like to call Mónica up front to tell how she felt in being bullied and then Sandra will come up to explain why she bullied Mónica so much. I know this will be hard for you, but the children need to hear both sides of the story and then we will have a few minutes of questions and answers. Is this clear?" All the students nodded.

Mónica was as red as a tomato when she approached the front. Miss Sánchez hugged her and whispered "You can do this. Just look at the picture in the back and talk to it."

"I, I felt my tummy very tight every time I thought of coming to school. Some mornings I would fall from the stairs on purpose hoping I would break a leg or something so I could stay home. Other days I would put my finger in my mouth to throw up so my mom wouldn't make me come to school because I didn't want to face Sandra. Many times, I knew the answer to Miss Sánchez's questions, but because all of you laughed at me, I wouldn't answer. No one played with me because I am shy, and I felt all alone and unappreciated. Every day I came to school was a terrible experience." Mónica ran to her desk and didn't notice that many of the children had tears in their eyes as they realized how bad they had made her feel.

It was Sandra's turn now. She slowly got up and covered her face with her hands as she stood in front of the class not knowing what to say. Miss Sánchez again came up to her and gave her a big hug while she whispered, "Sandra, you can do this. Tell the class what made you be so cruel to Mónica and how remorseful you feel. Everything will be ok, I promise."

"My dad left my mom and me not too long ago and I miss him very much." Sandra began to cry. "Mónica's dad also went away too not because he wanted to but because he passed away and I felt envious that her dad would have wanted to stay but was killed in an accident, but my dad chose to leave us." She paused again to catch her breath. "Instead of dealing with it, I took it out on Mónica because she didn't defend herself and took it quietly. When I was suspended for tripping Mónica once more, instead of having me expelled, Miss Sánchez spoke to Mr. Pérez asking him to let me participate with Mónica in a performance for the School's Celebration. As I came to know Mónica better and heard her sing, something inside me changed and I wanted to be her friend. Mónica, I am so sorry, can you forgive me?"

By this time both teacher and students were in tears. This had been a very touching moment and the girls had been able to find the courage to share their feelings.

Mónica ran up to the front and threw herself into Sandra's arms in response. The children stood up and clapped. Sandra and Mónica hugged each other even tighter and just laughed. Pretty soon the whole class was laughing with them.

"Ok class, settle down. Now we will have Mónica and Sandra answer your questions and then we will see how we can apply what we have read. We have ten minutes."

David raised his hand. "Yes, David, what is your question and who would you like to ask?"

"The question is for Mónica. Mónica, why didn't you stand up for yourself?"

"I didn't know how. I was afraid of being hurt, I guess," said Mónica.

Valentina was next in raising her hand. "This question is for Sandra. Sandra, why were you so mean to Mónica?"

"Because she didn't speak up and was easy to bully, but I don't feel that way anymore. She is my friend now and I will never hurt her again!" said Sandra.

Gustavo raised his hand. "This question is for Mónica. If I had been bullied as you were, I wouldn't become the friend of that bully, I would want him expelled! Why are you so nice to her after all she did?"

Mónica looked at Sandra and said, "Sandra is a good person. She was just too hurt and didn't realize how I felt, but now that she does, she is different and has a kind and thoughtful side. Besides, Miss Sánchez told me that love can fix anything. Right, Miss Sánchez?" asked Mónica.

"Yes, that is right. For bullying to stop we need to understand the bully's situation and confront him. It will not be easy, but it is necessary. Once we have done this, we need to show them love and compassion. People have reasons why they act like they do; they might not be right and certainly should not take it out on anyone, but they suffer just as much as those being bullied. You have to find a common ground and work from there," said Miss Sánchez.

"Ok class the time is up. I am sure you have many more questions for Sandra and Mónica which they will answer later. I want you to take this article and do some more research at home and come up with a plan so we will not have any more bullying in our classroom. Mónica and Sandra will then help us all with this project. Does this sound clear enough to everyone? You have a week to complete this assignment."

Once again, the children nodded and put the article away as Miss Sánchez was getting ready for the next subject. Miss Sánchez felt so happy things had turned out ok and that the children were apparently understanding what it meant to be a bully and how the ones being bullied were affected.

Chapter 6

The week had gone by quickly and now it was time for the children to present their findings. Miss Sánchez was really looking forward to some great ideas and plans to help those who were afraid to speak up for themselves. Mónica and Sandra had developed a beautiful friendship and were inseparable. They were the talk of the school, not only because they had performed so well, but because they had been able to overcome a sad situation and had both benefitted from the experience.

As Miss Sánchez walked into her classroom, she was surprised to see her students at their desks ready to start another school day. Everyone was rested and ready to go. They had had a long weekend and had enjoyed it, many of them going to the beach. Others had attended family gatherings, while others just stayed home and enjoyed their families. She had met up with friends and had had a great time.

"Good morning class. Since everyone is here and rested, we will go straight to our new project. How many of you had enough time to complete your assignment?" All hands went up.

"Wonderful! We will start then. I will call on you so don't raise your hands. Umm, ok let's start with Juanita. What did you find and how can you apply what you learned?"

Juanita stood at her desk and spoke. "My mom helped me find articles for children about bullying on the internet and this is what we found: 'Bullying in childhood is a major health problem that increases the risk of poor health, social and educational outcomes in childhood and adoles. . .adoles…'"

"Adolescence," interjected Miss Sánchez. "It means in your youth. Continue please, Juanita."

"'These not only affect those being bullied but the bullies themselves. They are now believed to continue into adulthood.' There are many, do you want me to continue?"

"No, thank you, Juanita. We will have someone else share their findings. However, before you sit down, please tell us what this means and what we can do about it."

"My mom said that it can cause us to get sick and that it affects us in school in the way we learn and act towards others. If we are not careful and stop at an early age, we can keep being bullies even when we are adults."

"Yes, Juanita. This is very true. Therefore, we must stop this right now and learn to be more accepting of other people."

"Ok let's see. Pablo, share your findings with the class please."

Pablo got up and went to the front of the class. "My dad helped me find the information. It says that children and even adults who are seen as being 'different' in any way are at great risk of being victims. Physical appearance can be the most frequently caused. The information we found also says that bullying exists in its traditional, sexual and cyber forms, which impact the physical, mental and social health of its victims. I think that we need to be more understanding and know that we are all different yet alike in many ways and should find something we can have in common."

"Good point, Pablo, thank you," said Miss Sánchez. "Next, we will hear from Natasha."

"Almost everything I found has already been said. The last thing I found was that nothing has been found to prevent bullying and that it is needed urgently."

"So, what would you recommend being done?"

"My mom and dad said that parents should talk about this at home and explain the consequences."

"That is very true, thank you, Natasha."

"Marcos, what do you have to say on the matter?"

"'Bullying is being mean to another kid repeatedly. It often includes teasing, talking about hurting someone, spreading rumors, leaving kids out on purpose, attacking someone by hitting them or yelling at them. Bullying does not always happen in person. Cyberbullying is a type of bullying that happens online or through text or emails. It includes posting rumors on Facebook, sharing embarrassing pictures or videos, and making fake profiles or websites.' I think if we get anything like that, we should show it first to our parents and then to our teacher and not spread it."

"Very good. Thank you, Marcos," said Miss Sánchez. "Idalia, you're up."

"Kids who are bullied can feel like they are: different, powerless, unpopular and alone. They have a hard time standing up for themselves. They think the kid who bullies them is more powerful than they are. Bullying can make them: sad, lonely, or nervous; feel sick; have problems at school; bully other kids. I think it is important to help other kids to feel accepted and loved. Maybe you could assign a school buddy to each of us to help one another."

"Idalia, that's a wonderful idea. How many are in favor? Wonderful class, I am so proud of you!"

"Ok, we have talked a lot of the kids being bullied, now let's talk about the bullies themselves and how it affects them. Ivan, do you have any information to share on this matter?"

"The kids that bully others do it for many reasons: they want to copy their friends; they think bullying will help them fit in; they think they are better than the kid they are bullying. Those who bully use power to hurt people. The bully may know a secret about the kid being bullied and use it against him. Like in Sandra's case, she acted out in anger because her dad left them. There are many reasons that are coming out. I think that just like Mónica did, we need as a group to stick together and not let any of our classmates be hurt in any way. We also need to investigate why bullies are the way they are and try to help them. Maybe they can change like Sandra did."

"That was very thoughtful Ivan and a very good suggestion. Good work!" said Miss Sánchez. "Ok, now that we have researched what bullying is, we need to come up with a plan. What are we going to do about it? Let's take a break and continue tomorrow. Right now, open your math books to page eleven and let's work on those problems. Thank you all for your contributions," said Miss Sánchez.

The kids worked quietly in their workbooks while Miss Sánchez observed them. She felt her heart was going to explode with gratitude. Presented the right way, kids can be very open to change and can appreciate and be aware of others' feelings. Now they would have to come up with a good, solid plan and Sandra and Mónica would be instrumental in carrying it forward.

As Sandra sat working on her math problems, she felt so bad for Mónica and all that she had put her through. She hadn't meant to be so mean; she just didn't know how to direct her frustration and anger. She hoped she could influence other bullies for good. Miss Sánchez was right and now she could see that she not only cared for Mónica, but she also cared and was mindful of all of them.

Meanwhile Mónica was also thinking about how much Sandra had changed and how she treasured her friendship. They were both helping each other become the best persons they could be. She would share all of this with her mom when she got home tonight.

When Mónica came home from school that day, she waited anxiously for her mom to come home so she could share all that was happening at school and how much she was now enjoying attending school. It was funny, a month ago she never wanted to go to school again and now she looked forward to it. Bullying was preventing her from being the happy child she was at school.

When her mom got home that night, she ran to her and gave her a big hug.

"What is this all about, are you ok?" said her mom. "Did you have a good day at school?"

"Oh, Mom, it was wonderful! We discussed bullying and how it affects both the bully as well as the one being bullied, and Miss Sánchez asked us to . . ."

She told her mom all about it and then her mom said, "See? I told you that all you had to do was find common ground. Sandra is a good kid; she just has been hurt too deeply by the person she trusted the most, her father. I am so glad you two are finally getting along and that she has understood the seriousness of the problem and has changed. Good for her and for you for being so willing to forgive and forget. I am so proud of you!" said Mom.

Chapter 7

"Good morning class," said Miss Sánchez. "We will finalize our discussion today on bullying. I hope all of you have suggestions so we can plan to share with the whole school at the assembly next week. This will be a special occasion as Mr. Pérez has invited the parents of all the children at school to attend since we will be talking about bullying and its harmful effects. The suggestions some of you presented yesterday were excellent and we will be sharing those next week. In fact, I was thinking that perhaps we could have several presenters and then finalize with Mónica and Sandra giving us their thoughts and feelings regarding their experience. What do you think?"

The class nodded their heads with excitement. Julio raised his hand. "Yes, Julio?"

"I was thinking that maybe after we all presented what we prepared, Sandra and Mónica could perform again in closing. They did it so well at the celebration! Besides, that would be an example of how bullying could be stopped and turned into something good."

"What a wonderful idea! What do you think class?"

Everyone clapped and shouted, "Yes, yes, that would be awesome!!"

"Well," said Miss Sánchez, "it looks like Sandra and Mónica will be performing again then. Girls, are you up for it?"

Mónica raised her hand. "I, I would love to if Sandra is willing to play for me. That way I wouldn't have to say anything in front of all those people." She blushed.

The children were tempted to laugh but Miss Sánchez gave them a warning look, so they remained quiet.

Sandra raised her hand with humility and said, "I would love to play for you. I really don't want to say anything either and this will show that we have become close friends and that there is hope for other kids that are struggling."

"Ok, then," said Miss Sánchez, "looks like we have part of the program done. Now let's get our presenters ready. Hum, let me see, we have less than an hour to present and then have Mónica and Sandra perform. I would like to have Natasha, Idalia Juanita, Pablo, Marcos, and Ivan to present what they learned like yesterday. The rest of you, please hand me your research and I will put it in a newsletter to hand out as people are coming into the auditorium. This way they will have all your thoughts. This is going to be great!"

Miss Sánchez collected their research and started to compile it as they worked on their Spanish test. This was going to be very interesting.

As the children finished and started leaving for recess, she stopped Sandra and Mónica and said, "Girls, have you thought of what you will be performing?"

Both girls looked at each other and shook their heads. "No, Miss Sánchez. Do you have any suggestions?" they asked.

"I just remembered a hymn the children at my congregation sing. It is called 'Love one Another.' Let me write down the lyrics, see what you think and if you like it, I can get the music, Sandra, so you can practice. It is very short, but sweet and I think it will really make a perfect closing."

Sandra and Mónica went to recess looking over the lyrics they had been given. When they came back from recess, they were both in agreement that this was the song they were to sing and play.

The days flew by and before they knew it, it was the day of the assembly. Miss Sánchez had asked her students to dress in their Sunday best and they were really looking sharp. They were all there backstage ready waiting for their turn to present. It was now their turn and Miss Sánchez quickly went out on stage to give a very brief introduction of the subject to be covered. The stage had been perfectly set up with chairs for all the presenters and a wireless microphone they would use to present.

Miss Sánchez took the microphone from Mr. Pérez and said, "Good afternoon, ladies and gentlemen. The subject of our presentation is regarding bullying and its effects on children. After our presenters have finished, we have a special treat for you. Sandra and Mónica will perform for you once more. Now I would like to call our presenters out to the stage."

The children came out and took their seats.

"First we will start out with Idalia and then go on to Ivan who will be our last speaker. Idalia . . ."

The children all gave good presentations and reflections. Miss Sánchez could see many parents agreeing with what was being said. When Ivan had finished his presentation, everyone clapped and continued clapping for a long time.

Miss Sánchez stepped up to the microphone once more and announced, "As promised, Mónica will sing 'Love One Another' a hymn from The Church of Jesus Christ of Latter-day Saints and Sandra will accompany on the violin." Sandra gave a brief introduction and Mónica started to sing:

> As I have loved you,
> Love one another.
> This new commandment:
> Love one another.
> By this shall men know
> Ye are my disciples,
> If ye have love
> One to another.

Again, as before, there was silence in the auditorium. Both children and their parents had tears in their eyes. This short hymn had touched their hearts and had blown away all those in attendance. These two wonderful little girls had come to appreciate, forgive, and love one another. That afternoon, both parents and children took away a clear perspective of what it meant to be a good student, friend, parent and above all a wonderful teacher who had taken it upon herself to care and love her students enough to help those struggling. This would be an event everyone would remember.